This
Book
Belongs
To ----- *Conway girls* -----

Grolier Enterprises Inc.
SHERMAN TURNPIKE, DANBURY, CONNECTICUT 06816

Book Club Edition

The Story Of The Good Samaritan

An ALICE IN BIBLELAND Storybook®

Written by Alice Joyce Davidson
Designed by Victoria Marshall

Text copyright ©1989 by Alice Joyce Davidson
Art copyright ©1989 by The C.R. Gibson Company
Published by The C.R. Gibson Company
Norwalk, Connecticut 06856
Printed in the United States of America
All rights reserved

A little girl named Alice
Had a neighbor named Miss Brothers
Who was always very busy
Doing what she could for others.

Alice liked to visit,
For it felt so peaceful there,
Sitting on the big, wide porch
Rocking in a chair.

She took her Bible storybook
While visiting one day,
And chose to read of Jesus
And a man who came His way.

"How can I get to heaven?"
Was a question from the man.
Jesus answered with a story
Of the Good Samaritan.

As Alice read her story,
The airmail bird stopped by.
He brought this note to Alice,
Then flew off in the sky:

"Reading is the magic key
To take you where you want to be."

Her book became a magic screen.
The screen grew tall and wide,
And Alice walked on through the screen
To Bibleland inside.

Alice was sent back in time,
And much to her surprise,
The story she was reading
Came to life before her eyes.

Between the city of Jerusalem
And far-off Jericho
There was a lonely, dangerous road
Where travelers feared to go.

A man was walking down this road.
Nobody was around,
When suddenly a band of thieves
Crept up without a sound.

They moved so very quickly,
There was nothing he could do.
The thieves took everything he had—
His clothes and money, too.

They hit him with a stick,
And then left him there to die
On that desolate and lonely road
Where few men traveled by.

Later on a priest came by.
He spied the poor man there.
He saw that he was beaten
And he had no clothes to wear.

But he didn't stop to help the man
Or see if he was dead.
The priest was in a hurry
So he crossed the road instead.

Soon a helper from the temple,
Called a Levite, came along.
He saw the injured man and knew
That something must be wrong.

This Levite didn't slow his pace
Or see what he could do.
He had to get to temple
So he hurried onward, too.

Now both the priest and Levite
Ignored the man in need,
Even though they were his neighbors,
They didn't do a helpful deed.

As nighttime came, a stranger
Trudged down that same road, too.
He saw the man, and instantly,
He knew what he must do.

"There's someone injured lying here,
A badly beaten man.
If he's alive, I'll help him
In any way I can."

The stranger was from Samaria
A fierce unfriendly land.
Yet the Samaritan stopped on the road
To offer a helping hand.

The Samaritan asked softly
If there was something he could do.
He put ointment on each wound he saw,
Then snow white bandages, too.

He helped him on his donkey.
And walked beside his injured load
Until he found a place to stop—
An inn beside the road.

All through the hours of the night
The Good Samaritan
Did everything that he could do
To help the injured man.

He called to the innkeeper
Early the next day
And said, "I can stay no longer,
I must be on my way.

"Here's a bit of money
For the man who's lying there.
Use it any way you can
To give the best of care.

"And if you need more money,
Spend what you must, and then
I'll pay you when I return
To this inn once again."

The time had come for Alice
To leave that Bible scene.
So she returned from Bibleland
And came back through her screen.

She left her neighbor's porch.
She put her book away
And thought about the lessons learned
In Bibleland today.

"From the story Jesus told
Of the Good Samaritan,
We learn to give our very best
To anyone we can.

"To belong to God's own family
I must learn to do for others
And be as kind and caring
As my neighbor Miss Brothers.

"If someone's sick or hungry,
I should never pass them by;
I should treat them like a brother
Jesus' story shows me why.

"I love God with all my heart
And I'll share the love He's given.
Isn't that the richest blessing
On earth as well as heaven?"

Copyrighted Material

Dear Catholic Friend

Copyright ©1961 Sword of the Lord Publications.
All Rights Reserved.

No part of this publication may be used or reproduced, stored in, or introduced into a retrieval system, or transmitted in any form or by any means (printed, written, photocopied, electronic, audio, or otherwise) without prior written permission of the publisher.

Sword of the Lord Publications
224 Bridge Avenue
Murfreesboro, TN 37129

swordofthelord.com

ISBN: 978-87398-152-1

All Scripture quotations are from the King James Bible.

Printed and Bound in the United States of America

DEAR CATHOLIC FRIEND

DR. JOHN R. RICE